The Wizards'

Apprentess

Publication Date: September 10, 2018

ISBN-13: 978-1-7750252-4-5

Chapter 1

In the midst of a verdant forest, home to magic and enchantment, there ran a broad sparkling stream, over which gently arched a low, wide bridge of pale wooden planks. Crossing this bridge, as they often did on such pleasant midspring afternoons, were two wizards, wiry but spry for their apparent age, with long white hair and beards; Mezuthelion, in robes of green, and Zithemander, draped in blue. They had long been such good friends that they were akin to brothers, and now they worked together to train a new youth; their apprentess, Tayarene.

She wore a thick robe of deep plum purple, with sleeves as capacious as the others' – but somehow she still managed to make the garment look feminine and playful. For playful she was, more than any other apprentice they'd had, and though she was a bit of a handful, they fondly joined in her sport, as she was the light of their day. They bantered and chuckled and pranked and capered, as they headed home to their cottage in the eastern half of the woods.

But the second wizard, Mezuthelion, was lagging back, and now he cast an uneasy glance over his shoulder. He scanned the edge of the woods behind them, but still saw nothing.

Zithemander noticed him lingering on the bridge, and paused to call back lightly, "What delays you?" Their apprentess was already some distance ahead.

"Just keeping an eye out for the monster that's rumoured to be about," he responded absently.

The other wizard seemed to take it as a matter of course, turning back to accompany Tayarene, and assuming Mezuthelion would soon follow.

Eventually, Mezuthelion hesitantly trailed after them until he was off the bridge, but slowed once more to look back.

Then, from the shadows beneath the trees, it emerged: a large wolflike creature, but with fur of a dull purple upon its back, and a grey underbelly.

Mezuthelion saw it with some relief. "Finally," he muttered; he'd been worried it wouldn't arrive on time. Tayarene was almost out of sight around the bend. "This is the girl," Mezuthelion told the wolf, looking toward Tayarene.

The wolf turned his dark eyes onto her, where they fixed with intent interest.

"As I said before," the wizard added, "you mustn't let her know who you are." With that, he continued on to catch up to his companions.

The creature slunk across the bridge after them, and passed unseen back into the forest.

***

Tayarene skipped along, leading the way up the path to the cottage. It was a cosy one-storey home, just big enough for the three of them, with pale wooden walls and a hipped thatch roof sprouting a little chimney. She twirled, her thick braid of long brunette hair sweeping about, and waited for the wizards to catch up.

Mezuthelion was still trailing behind, so she called to Zithemander as he neared. "Is it time for potions practice yet?" she prompted eagerly.

Zithemander chuckled. "Dear girl, we've only just gotten back," he protested mildly.

"I know, but I've been waiting to start since before we left."

Mezuthelion came up and clapped a hand on Zithemander's back. "A restorative elixir and you'll be good as new." A lighthearted tease that Zithemander was the slightly older of the two.

"If only we weren't fresh out," Zithemander remarked.

"We might as well brew one up. Let's try it outdoors this time, shall we?" Mezuthelion suggested, and eyed Tayarene with a twinkle in his eye. "We don't want a repeat of what happened last week."

She put the back of a hand on her hip playfully. "You know very well I wouldn't have dropped that explosive mixture if that dusty spellbook of yours hadn't made me sneeze," she countered.

Smiling, the wizards started heading past her for the house, and she turned to accompany them.

"You should really make better use of that enchanted feather duster..."

The three of them went into the sunny little cottage and ferried all the supplies outside, starting with a long table on which they set an assortment of bottles. Then Zithemander instructed Tayarene on which ingredients to mix together in what order and quantity, and Mezuthelion monitored her closely as she obliged. Lastly, she poured the blue liquid of one rounded beaker into the other, sparking a delightful puff of purple smoke that wafted up.

"Splendid!" Zithemander exclaimed, then paused. "Now...who wants to test it?"

The two wizards eyed each other cautiously sidelong. There was no telling what an untested concoction might do.

"She made it for you, after all," Mezuthelion ventured.

"Oh, very well," Zithemander conceded. "But I'll conduct a scan first to check." He swept his hand over the opening of the bottle, but didn't seem to sense any toxicity. He took it up and downed it in a few gulps, and Tayarene watched with anticipation. He smacked his lips as he set it down. "Ah! Not bad! I can feel some of the vitality returning to me already." Tayarene relaxed with glad relief. "I believe it could use a touch more pepberry juice next time, though."

Tayarene thought she glimpsed a pair of dark eyes watching her from the forest edge, but when she looked, all she saw was a blackbird perched in a tree there, probably made curious by all the potions.

Once noon came, Tayarene went to a small nearby glade that was still draped in the shade of the forest. She sat crosslegged on the grass at the base of a tree, and snacked on her luncheon. Just as she was almost done, there was a faint rustle in the bushes ahead, and out hopped a little auburn squirrel. It cocked its dark eye at her, and she smiled at it warmly.

"Hey there, little guy," she greeted in a delighted murmur. It started hesitantly stepping its way closer in little fits and starts. "Looking for some treats?"

Tayarene prompted, and held out a nut of offering.

It made one more bound right to the brink of her folded shins, then straightened up and took the nut from her fingers with his little handlike forefeet. Then he crouched on his haunches there to nibble on the treat, just as if he wasn't in human company.

Tayarene was curious. Usually they leapt away a safe distance with their prize before starting in on eating it. "You're remarkably tame," she observed. She extended a gentle finger to stroke on its head; it stayed where it was and let her pet him.

It finished up the rest of the nut, then promptly climbed up onto her lap, but didn't seem to be looking for more food. Tayarene lightly ran her hand down the smooth fur of its arched back, a few times. She couldn't get over how friendly it was.

It scampered up her arm, then settled itself on her shoulder, its bushy tail - curled behind it - brushing the side of her neck. Tayarene watched it with a smile. She'd never been so close to a wild critter. She reached up and petted it some more, and it seemed content to stay there.

The enchanted whistle sounded from back at the cottage, announcing it was one o'clock.

Tayarene looked its way, then turned back to the squirrel. "Alright, I'm getting up now," she said to it. She slowly rose to her feet, and the squirrel braced itself with both forefeet on her shoulder. Then it jumped off to cling to the tree behind her, craning its neck to look around at her. She smiled back at it as she headed away. "See you around."

The next morning, Tayarene stood in the cottage with the wizards, concentrating her gaze on her open uplifted hand as she envisioned the wooden sphere in the other room and tried to conjure it. It was supposedly easier starting out over short distances. Finally, the sphere appeared in her palm, and she grinned.

"Well done!" Zithemander congratulated.

Tayarene noticed a green light out the west window, and turned her head to look. The orb on its post above the wooden message box - which was shaped like a little house - was slowly glowing on and off, to indicate someone in town had sent a note using the box's twin. "Oh, there's a message for you, Mezuthelion," she said.

"Ah. I'll get it right now, then."

11

He flourished his hand, and was suddenly holding the selfsame scroll, with a green string tied around it.

Tayarene looked on in amazement. "How'd you do that? You haven't even laid eyes on that scroll before!"

Mezuthelion smiled. "Yes, but I'm familiar with the location it was in. Once you become experienced enough in conjuring, it's just a matter of knowing where to summon from." He unfurled the scroll and read it. "It seems the cooper has misplaced one of his tools. It should be a simple matter to find it with a locating spell." Mezuthelion left the scroll on the table, then they headed out to town, even though they'd just been there the day before. Such was the nature of being the local wizards.

After a leisurely half-hour walk, they arrived at the quaint village, nestled in the woods, with its sturdy buildings topped by steep slate roofs.

They paused in the square, and Mezuthelion turned to Tayarene. "This should be a fairly routine task. You can sit this one out if you like."

"Why not let her come along?" Zithemander put in.

"She's seen us do the likes of it before. And there wouldn't be much for her to do, since we haven't started her on locating spells yet."

"I'll just pick up some things from the market while you're gone," Tayarene offered. "We used up all the clover yesterday anyway."

"As you wish," Zithemander acquiesced. "See if you can get some sparrow feathers too." He handed her a few coins. They parted ways, and Tayarene continued on to where several stalls lined the street outside the shops.

She drifted along until she came to a stand selling fresh goods. She looked over the display, then pointed out her selections to the vendor. "I'll have the clover, the garlic, and the...sparrow feathers."

"That would make for an unusual stew," someone remarked beside her.

Tayarene turned to find a lad a bit older than her standing there. He had raffish black hair and dark eyes, and was exceedingly handsome, in an appealingly boyish sort of way. His maroon tunic was cut in a crisp style, with a diagonal grey stripe from each shoulder meeting on the chest.

Tayarene smiled. "It's for a potion," she explained brightly. "I'm getting supplies for the wizards while they see to a client. I'm their apprentess."

"A wizard girl?" he repeated, a twinkle of genuine interest in his eye as he regarded her. "Very impressive. You don't see one of those every day." There was nothing mocking in his tone, only admiration.

"I know - witchcraft is the more popular choice, but wizardry doesn't take that much more skill." Tayarene accepted the burlap bag of produce from the merchant and paid him. She continued on past the lad, and he fell into step beside her as she browsed along the row of tables.

"You looking for anything else?" he prompted. "I know this market like the back of my hand. I do odd jobs for the merchants here. Just say Rizorian sent you, and they'll give you a discount."

"Actually, I *could* use some pixie powder," she admitted. "But I haven't

15

been able to find any lately."

Rizorian squinted in thought. "Oh, yeah, I think I know someone who has some of that," he mused. "He mentioned he got a new batch of it just the other day."

They went to a shop past the stall at the very end, and Rizorian spoke with the merchant standing outside. As the man went in to get a sample, Rizorian looked at Tayarene. "Pixie powder, eh? That's used for love potions, isn't it?"

Tayarene chuckled, abashed. "It can also be made into a sleeping draught, of course, in the right combination."

When the merchant brought back a corked vial of sparkly dust, Tayarene thanked him heartily and gave him the necessary coins. Then she and Rizorian resumed walking.

Tayarene set the bottle in her bag,

and poked around in it to check if she had everything. "I...guess that's all I was going to get for now," she said, with a trace of regret.

They drifted to a stop, and Rizorian eyed her purchase bag. "You need to be getting back with those?"

"Neh, the wizards are using a locating spell to find someone's lost item. It could be a while."

Rizorian's eyes brightened a little.

"I should probably stay around here until they get back." She sat on the stone coping of a garden wall, the bag on her lap.

"I was thinking of staying around here too." He settled beside her.

Linking her hands around her knee, Tayarene leaned back and beamed up at the sky, where a hawk was gliding by high overhead. "The birds must have fun up there."

Rizorian looked over at her quizzically.

"Just imagine what it must be like, floating on currents of air. Levitation gives you some idea, but I'm not very good at it yet."

His eyebrows lifted. "Still, that's more than most people can do."

Tayarene chuckled. "True. It's not just birds that fascinate me, though. I admire animals of all kinds. They're so majestic and mysterious."

"Oh, absolutely," Rizorian agreed, turning toward her more. "Even though they can't speak, they still have emotions and personalities."

"Exactly! It would be unreasonable to think otherwise."

"And tame ones can be so affectionate. Sometimes I think they're

18

more in touch with their true selves than people are."

She watched him avidly, nodding, enthralled that they had something so passionately in common.

"There's nothing quite like the freedom of running on four legs." Then Rizorian proffered a wry smile. "Or at least, so I imagine," he added.

"Tayarene!" Zithemander's voice called, and she looked over to see the two wizards coming up to them from a side alley. She was a little disappointed. She'd hoped it'd take them longer.

She looked back at Rizorian as she got up. "See you later."

He slowly bloomed into a hopeful grin. "Really?"

Tayarene paused in her steps to head away. "I mean, since you're often around in the market, and all," she explained haltingly.

His eyes still twinkled. "Right."

Chapter 2

Tayarene set out into the forest north of the cottage to look for plants with magical properties. She spotted a cluster of dandybloom, with their soft yellow flowerheads facing the sky. She went over and knelt by them to pick them one by one. Their five-inch stems were thick but hollow, and spongy enough to be easily plucked.

The underbrush nearby stirred, and out peeked a dark brown ferret. It regarded her, then came shuffling closer, to nose curiously at her handful of flowers.

"These?" she prompted. "They're

called dandybloom. I'm gathering them for a potion."

The ferret turned tail and scampered away. Tayarene watched it go. *Oh well.* Maybe it had been scared off by her voice.

She turned back to her foraging. But not a minute later, the ferret came lolloping back up to her, holding up a dandybloom in its mouth. Tayarene looked at it with amused surprise. It looked so cute, like a little animal suitor, with its little teeth just peeking out around the stalk.

"For me? Oh - why, thank you!" she remarked, accepting it to add to her collection. She stroked the ferret's head. "Aren't you a clever little creature." Its whiskers quivered in such a way that it looked rather pleased with itself.

Tayarene got to her feet to start looking for another patch, and the ferret went scouting around to bring back whatever dandyblooms it found. Someone must have trained it to retrieve things.

Whenever she was in the woods, she always met some little animal or other – an oriole, a rabbit, an auburn bobcat – who came up to her and kept her company like she was one of them. Tayarene reckoned she must just have an affinity for animals. That, or the ambient magic in the area had made all the wildlife more friendly.

One time, when she was practicing levitation by herself, a grey gull alighted in front of her and cocked its head. Tayarene thought it was an unusual animal to be found in a forest. But maybe it was a frequenter of the rivers and ponds in the area. With her hands held out slightly from her sides, palms facing down, Tayarene tried to will herself up, by generating a sensation of resistance in her core. As her feet lifted an inch off the ground, the bird spread its wings and flapped them once so it was briefly suspended in the air too. Tayarene chuckled. She couldn't maintain her hovering for long, but after she came down she tried again. The gull beat its wings a few times, staying aloft in place longer, and Tayarene decided to take it as encouragement, as if the bird was showing her how to do it. She managed to rise a full foot up, and stayed there for nearly half a minute - but then she had to lower herself again, because sustaining it felt like holding her breath. But she kept at it, and the gull continued motivating her, until she figured out how to actually move forward while she floated, whereupon the bird even took wing and flew around her, and Tayarene laughed with exhilaration.

The next time Tayarene was in town, she continued ahead to sell some extra dandybloom powder, while the wizards shopped elsewhere in the market. There she spotted Rizorian again, and he gave her a winsome grin as he came over.

"Did I catch you on your way out?"

Tayarene smiled. "I have one more stop I could make. At town hall, to hear what the latest news is." It was halfway across town; plenty of time for a nice stroll and a chat.

Rizorian fell into step beside her. "I'll walk you there, then." As they started heading along the street, he went on, "So, you live with the wizards? Do you have any relatives nearby?"

"My aunt identifies enchanted objects here in town. Magic runs in my family. She's the one that saw I had more potential in me than that, and encouraged me to achieve it by becoming an apprentess. So I had to relocate here, even though that means I'm far away from where my parents live. What about you?"

He shrugged. "I never knew my family. I guess you could say I'm an orphan."

Tayarene looked at him with concerned sympathy. "Oh. Sorry to hear that."

"It's not so bad. I was raised by a nice old craftsman, until he passed a year ago. Been on my own since then; moved here. I'm staying in a boardinghouse on the southwest side of town."

In a momentary lapse of discussion, they passed a boy gossiping to his friends. "I heard the monster will drag off anyone who enters the woods! And then he eats their souls!"

Tayarene turned away, shaking her

head.

Rizorian looked over at her. "Those rumours worry you?" he prompted.

"No, I just don't think the monster is as bad as all that."

He studied her consideringly.

They soon arrived at town hall: a square two-storey building made of grey stone bricks, with a flat roof. They joined a ring of townsfolk outside it and listened to the herald proclaim reports about local happenings, as well as notable tidings of neighbouring villages and lands. Tayarene and Rizorian, at the back of the gathering, muttered humorous comments to each other about each piece of news. After five minutes they turned to head back, since the herald would only repeat his accounts once every hour. On their way, they kept talking until the last moment, when

Tayarene could see the wizards in the market ahead; then she waved back to Rizorian as he stayed behind.

Every time she visited town, she met up with him again, and they often became immersed in riveting conversation about their shared enthusiasms. They talked about anything and everything; they laughed and shared updates about their days, and soon came to be close friends. They got along so well, and she really liked him.

One day, Tayarene was heading up the street, coming back from an errand the wizards sent her on to help with a client. She neared a circle of several youths her age, and overheard one of them saying, "You really think there's a monster, Suziri?"

Looking at them, Tayarene slowed to listen.

"Of course!" replied the blonde girl with her back to Tayarene. "There've been countless sightings of it. That monster has been terrorizing the town long enough. It's about time something was done about it."

Tayarene stepped in. "What makes you think it's a monster, and not just a regular animal?"

Suziri looked at her. "What else could it be, when it's a huge wolf with purple fur? It's undoubtedly vicious."

"When have you heard of it ever hurting anyone?" Tayarene countered.

"It matters not whether it's been seen attacking yet. It's an abomination. It needs to be eradicated."

Tayarene was taken aback by the extreme notion. "It's probably just some poor creature that's trying to mind its own business. You shouldn't judge it based solely on its unusual appearance."

Suziri sneered. "Taking the beast's side? You must be one of those sappy animal-lovers that wouldn't hurt a mouse even if it ate all the grain in your cellar."

Tayarene's mood darkened. "That's right, I wouldn't. There are humane ways to deal with inconvenient creatures. I'd cast a warding spell to keep it out of the cellar."

Suziri scoffed, turning back to the others. "Well, not all of us can just use magic to solve our problems. Sparing one mouse just leaves it free to raid someone else's cellar. *I* say, getting rid of that menace *before* it strikes would be doing everyone a favour." And she and her friends walked off before Tayarene could get a word in.

The apprentess balled her fists, stewing.

Chapter 3

Tayarene was passing by the message box the next day when she noticed its orb flashing red. *An emergency!* She rushed over to open the glass-paned door. Inside sat a small scroll tied with purple string, meaning it was addressed to her. She pulled the twine off and unrolled it.

Apprentess Tayarene,

Your aunt has become trapped in a magic sleeping mirror that can only be operated from the outside. No one else in town has the abilities to help.

Her stomach dropped. "Oh no,"

she breathed. The longer someone was in the mirror, the closer they would get to falling into an enchanted slumber. Tayarene looked around. Both of the wizards were gone foraging for herbs in the forest. It would take too long to go looking for them, or wait for them to get back. She set the scroll back in the message box and left its door open, so the wizards would notice it when they returned. She would have to go to town herself. But with the time it took to get there afoot, it might still be too late.

Just as she was wishing for a means of swift transport, a form stirred beneath the dappled shade of the trees, and out stepped a handsome stallion of a rich bay coat, watching her as it came to stand in the middle of the clearing. Tayarene stared at it for a moment, wondering what a wild horse could be doing out here in the woods – then she turned thoughtful. She carefully approached it, and stroked a gentle hand onto its velvety snout, which was received just as if it were a fully tame mount. She looked into one of those large, dark eyes. "Will you let me ride you?" Tayarene asked it in a whisper, and the stallion gave a decisive snort. Deciding to take her chances, she swung up onto its back, and nudged its side with her knee to set it charging onward to their destination.

Fifteen minutes later they galloped into town, and the horse clomped to a halt so she could dismount. Tayarene started striding purposefully in the direction of the boardinghouse, and the stallion trotted loyally after her. "Rizorian!" she called in desperation. She cast about for any sign of his face amidst those of the villagers, peering down alleyways as she went past. Without slowing, she even asked a passerby if they'd seen him around lately, but they hadn't. A blackbird flew overhead and disappeared behind the rooftops as she kept calling, "Rizorian!"

The lad himself suddenly emerged from a side street before her, looking surprised that she was calling him, but attentively concerned as to her urgent tone of voice. "What is it?" Oddly, he seemed somewhat out of breath.

Tayarene was so relieved to find him that she briefly set her hands on his chest as their meeting brought her to an abrupt stop. "It's my aunt! She's suffered a magical mishap! I need you to go get an anti-magic pendant from the market." Her aunt always wore one while inspecting unidentified artifacts to prevent these kind of incidents. But then that left the question, how had it happened?

"Of course," Rizorian agreed

earnestly.

Tayarene looked over her shoulder, but the bay stallion was no longer there. Frowning, she scanned around. "Where'd he go?" she wondered.

"Where'd who go?" Rizorian prompted.

"The horse that brought me here."

He paused for an uncertain moment. "Do you need a ride? I can get another mount for you –" he offered.

"No, never mind," she muttered. "I just thought he'd still be here when I need it."

Rizorian compressed his lips, with a very inscrutable expression of dissatisfied hesitation.

Tayarene looked at him again. "But go, hurry," she urged. "Meet me at my aunt's shop." She turned to hasten away, and Rizorian jogged off in the opposite direction.

She raced to her aunt's place and burst in the door. Inside the stand mirror ahead, her aunt looked up, then pressed her hands on the glass with an expression of desperate relief, and mouthed her name. Tayarene rushed up to her. "Aunt! Are you okay? How do I get you out?"

Her aunt frowned. Then her mouth moved, but no sound came through. Her aunt pointed to the frame, where there was a raised, carved disc. Then she made a turning motion with her hand. Tayarene tried to rotate the disc, but it wouldn't budge. Meeting her aunt's eyes, she shook her head and shrugged in a helpless gesture.

Her aunt pointed insistently to something behind Tayarene, then moved her hands like she was opening a book. Tayarene looked over her shoulder, and

36

went to consult the volume laying open on the table there. It was a reference of antique magical objects, catalogued by her aunt, and it was open on the page about magic mirrors. Tayarene found the illustration of the particular kind her aunt was in, and read the notes on how to release a captive from it.

Rizorian came dashing in the open door, bringing the pendant to Tayarene. As she put it on, he caught his breath for a bit. He looked at her aunt in the mirror with concern, then turned to Tayarene. "Is there anything else I can do?"

"Looks like I'll need you to put this orb in that mirror frame at the exact same moment I turn the disc on the other side." She handed him the polished darkwood sphere she'd found on the tabletop.

She turned back to the mirror to see her aunt sitting sagged against the glass, blinking drowsily with her head nodding.

"No! Don't fall asleep!" Tayarene exclaimed. She wasted no time in starting the process. She rested one hand on the disc while she held the book in the other, and from it she read the incantation. "Segatsoh ruoy esaeler!" Just as she turned the disc to the right, Rizorian set the orb back in its socket. The glass became insubstantial, and her aunt slumped out. Rizorian darted to catch her under the shoulders before her head hit the floor.

Tayarene set the book down and knelt by her aunt, studying her face with worry, but her aunt's eyes remained closed. "Come on, Aunt, wake up," she pleaded, lifting her aunt's hand in hers and patting the back of it. But she didn't stir.

Rizorian looked up at Tayarene for instructions.

She ran a hand back over her own hair, staring at her aunt. "I'll have to make an antidote potion," she muttered. *Even though they don't always work.* "Let's get her on the bed."

Tayarene took her aunt's ankles while Rizorian hefted her up under her back, and together they shuffled her over to the cot by the side wall. They made sure she was laid out comfortably – then Tayarene went bustling about gathering supplies, bringing them back to the table to start mixing them together in a very precise sequence and measure. She had Rizorian help out when he could, fetching bottles from the shelves or holding things when she needed more than two hands. He obliged silently so as not to break her concentration, and mostly watched her work, solemn yet fascinated; but once she caught him looking at her with deep admiration.

When she was finally done, she took the blue potion over and held it near her aunt's nose so she would breathe in the billowing vapour. After a full minute, Tayarene withdrew the bottle and waited with bated breath. But even after several minutes, there was no change. "It's not working," she whispered. She got a sinking feeling. What if she hadn't done the potion right? She'd never had to make one for something this important before.

"Maybe it just needs more time to set in," Rizorian suggested.

Tayarene nodded, setting the bottle on the bedside table. "You're right. Some enchanted sleeps take longer to wake from than others." She tried to calm her nerves by reminding herself of that.

She leaned back on a low bureau with her hands on the edge, watching her aunt. Rizorian came over to settle likewise beside her. After a while, he set his hand on top of hers. A poignant tenderness rose in her. Tayarene interlaced her fingers with his. She was very grateful that he was staying with her in her time of crisis, just to be there for her. He was a true friend.

The better part of an hour passed, but still her aunt showed no signs of coming to. Then the grand clock behind them chimed noon, and Tayarene looked over her shoulder. She turned to Rizorian. "Do you need to have luncheon?" she prompted.

He met her eyes. "I'd rather stay."

She smiled. "If nothing's happened in an hour, it's not likely to anytime soon. I'd feel better if I knew you'd eaten."

Rizorian hesitated for another moment. "All right. But I'll bring you back

41

something." He rose and went out the back.

A few minutes later, the sound of Mezuthelion calling her name carried through the open front door. Tayarene leapt to her feet and ran outside.

The two wizards came hustling up the street. "We came as soon as we found the message," Zithemander said, taking her hands.

"I didn't get her out soon enough," Tayarene lamented as they went inside. "I gave her an antidote, but she still hasn't woken."

The wizards crossed to her aunt's bedside, and Zithemander hovered his hand over her forehead to perform a magical assessment, while Mezuthelion double-checked with Tayarene that she'd made the potion with all the right ingredients.

"You did well," Zithemander told her. "There's nothing more to be done now, but wait for the potion to take effect."

Tayarene wrung her hands, monitoring her aunt. "I should stay here with her, until I know she's alright." If she didn't wake, it would mean Tayarene's potion hadn't been effective after all, and the wizards would have to administer another one – but by then, more time would have passed, and it would be all the harder to revive her at all.

"Shall we remain with you?" Zithemander offered.

She paused. "No, you don't have to. I'll be alright."

Mezuthelion set a hand on her back. "You're sure?"

Tayarene nodded. "I'll send you a message if I need anything."

Zithemander patted her shoulder as they headed past her for the door. "Take heart, dear girl. All will be well."

Once they'd left, Tayarene sighed and pulled up a chair beside her aunt's bed. Leaning on her knees, she clasped her hands and set her chin down on her fingers, eyes steady on her aunt. She was going to stay here overnight if she had to.

Chapter 4

The band of black-clad youths chased the monster through the dark forest, only catching fleeting glimpses of it between the trees; a flash of purplish fur here, a swish of tail there. They fired arrows at it whenever they got a chance, but aiming at a barely-seen moving target at night, while running, rarely yielded more than a hit trunk or pierced ground. One time, however, after a shot flew out of sight, a yip of pain sounded from the blackness ahead.

"I think I nicked it!" the lad responsible yelled triumphantly.

The rest of them kept charging forward in anticipation, and broke out into a moonlit clearing – but there was no sign of the monster. They straggled to a halt in the middle of the open space, casting about everywhere, and several of them fanned out to search the treeline. In the ensuing silence, Suziri listened hard for any hint of its presence, and heard a faint swishing within a pond on the right.

"What was that?" she demanded, pointing imperiously.

One of her boys knelt down by the pool's edge, and leaned forward on his hands to peer into the water. "It's just a fish," he reported dismissively.

"It might have seen the monster go by," Suziri reckoned. "Let's take it to the town witch and have her scan its memory." It was a long shot, but she would take any lead she could get. Their hunt was at an end anyway; there would be no finding the monster again tonight.

***

Tayarene was strolling down the main street of town, hands in the capacious pockets of her robe. Waiting for her aunt's situation to improve kept her anxious, and she hadn't been able to sleep. She glimpsed a motion ahead, and glanced up in time to see a stream of dark-clothed figures dash across the street. She frowned, and hurried after them to see what was going on. She rounded the corner into a narrow side alley, and as she got closer to them, she recognized the blonde girl bringing up the rear.

"Suziri!" the apprentess barked, and the girl glanced sharply over her shoulder. She held a clear glass canteen of water with a small orange fish swimming in it, and several of her young cohorts had ebony bows slung across their backs. Tayarene didn't know what they were up to, but by the looks of it, it couldn't be anything good.

"Stay back, animal lover!" Suziri disparaged scathingly. Her team of about twelve had paused by the roofed back porch of a bungalow, and now she followed them in scaling up the porch's fence-pillar, onto the roof tiles of the house.

The apprentess caught up to where they had been, and unthinkingly scrambled up after them. She started chasing the gang across the low slope of the slate tiles, but by that time they were already halfway across.

They ran up a plank that led to the flat rooftop of a two-storey shop, which stood several yards away from the building they were on. When the last one had crossed, he kicked the board off so it fell to the cobblestones below with a clatter that jarred the complacent stillness of the night.

Tayarene lifted her arms from her sides and rose into the air, levitating herself across the gap to land on the rooftop. She pursued them across it, but Suziri turned back to face her just short of the edge, and Tayarene paused too, still in a ready stance.

"That monster deserves to be put down," the girl called heatedly. "You won't stop us!" She cast the jugful of water, fish and all, into the square planter in the corner. Then she whirled after her posse and leapt off the building, dropping from sight.

The apprentess rushed after her,

and stopped at the ledge to peer over it, down at the dark street below – but the lot of them were nowhere to be seen. Then Tayarene hastened to check on the fish, which was still moving, in a small puddle that had accumulated in the corner of sunken dirt. With a wave of her hand she conjured a jar out of thin air, and carefully scooped the fish up into it. She was skilled enough by now that she could summon it all the way from her aunt's house. "Don't worry," she murmured to the fish. "I'll get you back home."

Tayarene went to the north side of the roof and stepped off the edge, holding one hand out to float down until her feet touched the ground. Then she headed east out of town, and held up a glow-orb to light the way on her fifteen-minute walk to the stream. There she knelt and poured the fish into the dark waters.

~~~

Tayarene straightened in her chair and rubbed her eyes. Morning sunlight streamed into her aunt's shop, but her aunt still lay there on the cot. Tayarene was about to look away when she thought she saw her aunt stir. Then her aunt inhaled and opened her eyes. Tayarene's heart leapt.

"Aunt!" Tayarene cried, springing up to sit on the bed by her aunt's side as she levered herself up. "I was afraid my antidote hadn't worked!"

Her aunt wrapped Tayarene in an embrace. "Oh, I had no doubt you could do it."

Tayarene backed up to look at her. "How did it happen? You're always so careful. Why weren't you wearing your anti-magic pendant?"

"It's the strangest thing," she mused. "I haven't been able to find it lately. I found my window open one day, when I hadn't left it that way. I think some hooligans broke in and stole it. But what they'd want it for, I don't know."

The first thing that came to Tayarene's mind was Suziri and her gang. Could they have taken it to use as a precaution against the monster, even though there was no reason to believe it could use magic on anyone? She felt a flare of indignation. She wouldn't put it past them, what with them sneaking around at night in their dark garb. She just couldn't recall if she'd seen Suziri wearing one. But if they'd put her aunt through all that peril just for their baseless vendetta... Tayarene had to tell the wizards about them. Someone had to make sure they didn't continue their mischief, especially if they were going to be terrorizing innocent animals like that fish in the process, for whatever purpose.

Tayarene met her aunt's eyes again. "Couldn't you have gotten another pendant at the market?"

"They didn't have any the last time I checked. And that mirror's been on a rush order for days, as requested by its owner. Besides, we used to identify without them, back in the old days before anti-magic pendants were made. It's always been a risky business."

"Well, here, have this one," Tayarene offered, lifting her own pendant off and settling it over her aunt's head instead. "I'll see if I can find out what happened to yours."

Tayarene checked to make sure her aunt was all back to normal now, with no narcoleptic side effects from the enchanted sleep. After she helped her aunt get settled and saw if she needed anything, her aunt told her she'd be fine.

Tayarene went to the message box at the east end of town and wrote a quick note to the wizards.

My aunt's awake, and doing well! I'll be heading back soon. Tell you more when I get there.

Tayarene

After she sent it, she started off toward the market to look for Rizorian. She spotted him in the midmorning crowd with his back mostly to her, and headed for him.

He turned his head her way, and she was alarmed to see a thin cut running across his right cheek. "Rizorian!" she breathed, hurrying over to him. She lifted a hand to hover near it, but he winced and averted his face as if belatedly trying to hide it from her. "What happened?"

"It's just a scratch," he explained lightly, with a bit of a grimacing smile. "Hunting accident."

She met his eyes curiously. "I didn't know you hunt."

"I don't," he admitted, but she was too preoccupied with her concern for him to bother with puzzling out what that meant.

"Here, let me mend it for you," Tayarene murmured. She took a small orb of smooth aquamarine out of her robe, and rolled it between her cupped palms until it glowed with healing power. Then she raised one hand and lightly touched her fingertips to just below the wound, conveying the magic to it. It closed up in a matter of seconds, leaving only smooth skin in its place, and she lowered her hand

55

in relief.

Rizorian's mouth promptly spread into a more customary insouciant beam. "Thanks!" he remarked brightly. "1 knew you wouldn't let anything happen to such a pretty face."

Tayarene smiled easily too, and tucked the sphere away again. "Anyway, 1 should be getting home now, but 1 just came to say my aunt is fully recovered."

"Oh! Great! See, 1 told you there was nothing wrong with your potion." The day before, Rizorian had come back after lunch and kept her company for a few more hours, but then Tayarene had reassured him that he didn't have to spend the whole day there. He must've gotten the scratch sometime between then and now.

"Oh, and 1 forgot to reimburse you for the pendant you got for me," she added, starting to dig out a coin from her pouch.

But Rizorian waved the thought away. "Nah, don't mention it! It was the least I could do."

Tayarene paused, then smiled again. "Well, thanks so much for all your help," she finished warmly. "It means a lot." Rizorian just kept looking at her gently with a faint smile, and she wondered if he was thinking about how they'd held hands, and what that meant to her. She turned to go before she could become bashful. "See you."

Once she was on the eastward path into the woods, she kept it in mind to tell the wizards about Suziri. When she neared the cottage, they came outside to meet her.

"There's a gang of young hunters in town," Tayarene told them urgently as she ran up. "They're going after the creature they call the monster." They both looked concerned – but it might have been more for the youngsters doing the hunting than for the monster. "We have to do something to get them to stop."

The two exchanged a deliberative glance. "Our assistance hasn't been requested in this matter," Zithemander replied regretfully. "It is not our place to interfere."

As he turned and left the conversation, Tayarene appealed to the other one. "Mezuthelion," she pleaded.

He started heading past her too, but in the direction of town. "Worry not, child," he murmured with an absent pat on her arm. "I will see to it that no harm comes of this."

Her face warmed into a smile of grateful relief. Then she followed

Zithemander inside to fill him in on the details of her aunt's recovery.

Mezuthelion was gone for several hours, but as the afternoon became late, Tayarene went out and sat on a stump to watch for him, too expectant to do anything else.

When she finally saw Mezuthelion returning, she got to her feet and hastened to meet him. "How'd it go?"

"Suffice it to say, I led them to believe that the monster had moved on to another town. They were so zealous in their goal that they relocated themselves there. I doubt we'll be hearing from them again."

Tayarene broke into a grin, and hugged the wizard sidelong.

Chapter 5

As Tayarene stepped out of the cottage, the message box orb glowed purple. *For me?* Tayarene hurried over to check it. She undid the purple twine and unfurled the scroll, to see it was from Rizorian. Her heart warmed at the thought of him.

Been a few days since I saw you. Just felt like chatting. Figured, why wait, when I could send a message? I was just wondering, what do you think would happen if you took a sleeping potion right after a levitating potion? Would you end up sleepfloating?

Tayarene grinned. Then, feeling playful, she took a slip of parchment from the enclosed compartment beside the box and wrote a reply of her own with a peacock-feather quill, which was enchanted so it never ran out of ink.

Actually, it might give you dreams of being suspended on clouds.

She closed the door to send it through, and it disappeared in a flash of light. She waited around for a few minutes, bobbing on her toes, hoping Rizorian was still there at the town message box to see it. Sure enough, a second scroll soon showed up.

What, you mean mixing potions can give you sweet dreams on demand? Then give me a youth potion and I'll sleep like a baby!

Tayarene giggled, then composed another response.

***

The two wizards stood some distance behind, watching their apprentess.

"She's been messaging for over an hour," Zithemander muttered. But there wasn't much emphasis in it.

Mezuthelion was smiling fondly. "Ah, let her enjoy it," he murmured.

***

Tayarene sat at the base of a tree after luncheon, in the same clearing she often frequented.

An auburn fox trotted out into the open. Its paws were black, as were its ears and the tip of its bushy tail. It idly nosed at the ground a bit, then came padding over to her, and settled itself onto its haunches in front of her.

The apprentess smiled. "You're quite well-mannered." She stroked her hands over the fluffy fur on either side of its face, studying it thoughtfully. "You remind me so much of another creature," she murmured.

It gazed at her for a moment with those dark eyes, eyes that she was sure she had seen on every other animal she'd met with lately... Then she watched as the fox morphed before her eyes, into that very same auburn squirrel she had just been thinking of. Tayarene drew in a soft gasp. They weren't just wildlife, none of them; it was a single creature, that could change its form at will, into anything that was part of the animal kingdom. But what kind of creature could do that?

"What *are* you?" she whispered.

The squirrel's tail twitched. It turned and scurried a few feet away before facing back to her. Then its form changed and grew, until there stood before her a wolflike creature the size of a bear, with purple and grey fur. Tayarene's mouth slowly dropped open. The creature everyone called the 'monster'.

But wait...that meant her animal friend and the monster were one and the same. Yet, in all its forms, it had been so playful and friendly and harmless, even helpful. He could've changed into the monster at any time and attacked her when she was vulnerable, but he never had.

Then Tayarene's face bloomed into a grin. "I knew you weren't a monster!" she cooed. "You're just a shapeshifter!" Encouraged by her response, he came back over, and laid himself out before her. "For all we know, you could have the spirit of a mouse!" He set his muzzle down on her knee, looking up at her with endearing eyes. She stroked his head between the lowered ears. "You wouldn't hurt anyone, now would you?"

He nuzzled against her midriff, and Tayarene wrapped her arms around his shaggy neck, hugging him close and snuggling her face into his warm thick fur.

No wonder those animals had all been so familiar with her. They'd already known her from before! This meant every moment she'd spent with them, all the fondness of each interaction, she could now attribute to one individual!

From then on, since she knew what the creature could do, he often changed into different forms on the spot, and Tayarene had even more fun with that.

On one occasion, she ran around with him trotting as a fox by her side. When she tossed a kerchief into the air, he turned into an owl in mid-stride and flew ahead to catch the cloth in his talons, then banked and came gliding back to her. As she took the kerchief, he alighted on her arm, then morphed into that same dark-brown ferret. Smiling, Tayarene held him close and nestled her cheek against his furry little face. He was an animal companion like she'd always wanted - but even better than just a pet, because he could shapeshift into all kinds of creatures. And because he was her friend.

One afternoon, Tayarene went down to the stream wearing only a linen top and shorts, so she wouldn't get her robes wet. She waded calf-deep into the cool current and bent over, reaching a hand in to look for fish scales amidst the smooth pebbles of the riverbed.

On the opposite bank, a dark brown otter bounded over, and rose up on its hind legs with its forefeet tucked on its chest.

Tayarene met its merry dark eyes, and smiled. "Hey there, you," she greeted. It seemed that no matter where she went, she'd never be without company.

The otter promptly dove into the water, did a few fluid twirls, then bobbed back up, looking at her expectantly.

"I can't play right now, I have collecting to do," she protested lightly.

The otter floated around on its back, chittering playfully.

Tayarene chuckled. "Oh, all right, just for a little bit!" she conceded, and went splashing after the otter. They chased each other around, sometimes with Tayarene swimming too. Or she floated on her back and the otter made a swimming jump right over her middle. He even climbed up on her, and she stroked his wet fur, then hugged him.

But, much as she enjoyed their romps, eventually she had to get back to the task at hand. So as to spend that much more time with her, the otter helped her gather what she was looking for, as it had before, since it was clearly even more intelligent than a regular animal. She welcomed his companionship, and wished it could be for the whole day. His assistance must mean he cared about her.

Every time Tayarene headed to town with the wizards, she looked forward to meeting with Rizorian. She was always glad to see him, with his handsome face and cheery expression. They were even closer now after the episode with her aunt. They also started going to events like craft festivals and potion contests, in which case Tayarene stayed longer while the wizards continued home. By the time she'd known Rizorian for three weeks, it was like they'd been best friends for years.

Upon parting with him one time, Tayarene turned and started away, harbouring an ebullient smile. A warm glow of affection still filled her heart. Could it mean...she was in love with him? She was in reverent awe of the possibility. This was the first time she'd ever felt like this about someone!

One hot summer day, Tayarene went to her favourite skinnydipping pond in the forest. She stopped by the edge and peeled her robes off over her head, letting them drop in a crumple to the ground beside her. Then she slowly lowered herself into the lukewarm water, which was cooler than the air by just enough to be refreshing. She continued in until her whole bare body was submerged, with just her head above, as she lazily stirred her arms. It sure beat all the work of drawing a bath.

The surface rippled nearby, and a little orange fish poked its head up. Tayarene was delighted to see it. It was the same fish she had rescued from Suziri. And now she recognized its twinkling dark eyes. "That was you, too?" It was a good thing Tayarene had helped it. He probably hadn't wanted to morph into a different animal in front of the hunters, lest he reveal his identity. Suziri must not have known she'd had the very 'monster' she was seeking, right in her grasp!

The fish ducked under again, and soon Tayarene thought she could sense the slight swishing of its passage through the pool around her.

She felt something small and warm and smooth brush very lightly across the sole of her foot, then her right thigh...then her waist...and arm, and hand, exploring her naked body little by little. It felt very sensual, and somehow she got the feeling that the fish intended it that way, and was enjoying her sultrily too.

Tender feelings stirred within Tayarene, and she wondered; how could she be in love with an animal? But she felt a deeper connection with it, as if its soul was more than just that of a creature.

The fish resurfaced in front of her, eyeing her softly as it slowly drifted around her. Then it morphed into a sea lion, and Tayarene stroked a hand over its sleek back as it glided past.

She remembered Rizorian, and felt a bit of a guilty twinge. How could she feel as much for the creature as for him? It wasn't fair to either of them. Neither knew she was always meeting with one behind the other's back; each probably thought they were her only special friend. They'd never been in the same place at the same time before. Maybe she should tell them. But what would Rizorian think, if she said she had feelings for an animal? It wasn't like she could choose the creature instead of a human. And would the shapeshifter be hurt, if it thought she was favouring a person over it? She didn't know what to do. But she couldn't stop seeing either of them without explanation, not until she decided.

Chapter 6

As the summer went on, Tayarene continued to visit the forest's many waterways in her swim clothes, just for fun and cooling off. She was invariably joined by her animal friend, who often changed into a dolphin, as it seemed that was one of his favourite forms. It was one of her favourites, too. They swam together in the streams, which were just deep and wide enough for him to be afloat in. Tayarene sidestroked alongside him, or behind his fluke, or sometimes held onto his dorsal fin so she could drift along with him as he glided through the water. When they reached larger ponds, they played around more rambunctiously, splashing each other and doing tricks and even maneuvering underwater. They were like two dolphins in a pod.

Late one afternoon, after spending hours with him, Tayarene idled near him in a secluded pond. The air, thick with pleasant heat, was gradually cooling, the sun just beginning to turn ruddy as it reflected off the calm rippling surface.

The dolphin gradually drifted over to her, sidling his rounded beak in over her shoulder, and Tayarene tenderly wrapped her arms around his barrel, just above the flippers, as if they were sharing a real hug. He slowly stirred his fluke, tail curved so they started rotating in place, floating together in the warm water. Gently Tayarene closed her eyes, resting her head on the side of his, letting herself be carried in the tranquil moment.

Then, she heard a very quiet sound; that of a soft, young male voice, as if it was whispering by her ear – or in her mind.

If only I was in my human form, and able to speak... it mused absently to itself, wistful. *Then I could tell her how much I love her... If only she could hear me...*

Tayarene was filled with excitement as she realized she must be tuning into his thoughts. "But I *can* hear you!" she told him in hasty reassurance, and the dolphin backed up to look at her in wonder.

You can? There was a sparkle of hope in that dark eye. But then its expression turned solemn. *Then...there is something else I must tell you.* His mental tone was heavy with regret. *I only have a few hours left to live.*

Tayarene stared at him, feeling her stomach drop with dreadful shock. "What?" she breathed.

He lowered his eyes. *I will soon perish unless I find the kiss of true love; I only had till I turned eighteen. That time will be upon me any hour now.*

Her eyes began to mist with tears. "Oh, my dear friend!" she whispered. Would that she or the wizards could lift his spell, but she knew that whatever required true love's kiss had no such loopholes. Then she had a thought. "Wait - let me do it! You can turn into your human form, right?"

I already begin to weaken. He was looking increasingly weary, his head low in the water, his eyelids half-closed. *I'm unable to transform now, unless I come to be on dry land.*

"Then here, let me help you ashore!" she offered with alacrity, hastening back until her feet had a purchase on the soft floor of the pond, while using her hands, still on his flippers, to tow him afloat through the water. She assisted in pulling him up onto solid ground, until he was beached fully out of the shallows. He lay there inertly, and Tayarene knelt by his side to watch and wait with worry, while her wet clothes and braid dripped onto the sand.

As the sun dried his skin, his form began to shift and change – until there lay on his back a clad human lad whom she instantly recognized.

What delight, what relief, to see that he was none other than Rizorian! All her guilt was banished, for her two loves were one!

He smiled faintly at her expression.

"Surprise," he murmured.

Of course; the voice of his thoughts had sounded familiar, but she had just been too caught up in the urgency of the moment to make the connection. And those dark eyes were the same, with their dear sweetness, with their knowing twinkle. She was sure now that she would make a viable candidate for the task, for it was clear that not half, but all of her heart belonged to him.

Tayarene set her hands on the sand before her knees, regarding his recumbent form. "Here goes," she murmured.

Then she slowly leaned down, hovering over his face, and sidled her mouth up to his to give him a very tentative, inexperienced kiss. His lips were a bit cold, and still wet from the water, but her heart sang to be so close to him, to be connected with him that way – and though he was still too weak to move much, she could tell he felt the same avidity to stay united with her.

When she backed away, she studied him anxiously. "Did it work?" she whispered.

"No it didn't," he murmured, resigned.

"Of course it did!" she insisted with bolstering conviction. "It must have!" She paused, then repeated more tenuously, "Right?" At least, she really hoped so. She felt a trace of uneasy doubt now. If it hadn't, that meant that they weren't really meant for each other...and that would be beyond devastating. Even worse, it would mean he had no one near that could save his life on time – and then he would be gone, and...her love for him couldn't stand that painful thought.

"Maybe we should...try it again," Rizorian muttered, voice still faint. "...just to make sure."

She was all too keen to oblige, if it would increase the chance of success. So she bent down with her forearms laid against his chest, and kissed him again, with all the concerned affection she felt inside - but from there, it turned into a lengthier thing.

Rizorian absently wrapped his arm around the back of her shoulders, tilting with her slightly to one side. Held close atop him, Tayarene could feel all the adolescent muscles of his chest and torso and arms, surrounded by his warm body. He now participated actively in the leisured kissing, as reluctant to leave off her lips as he was eager to hold onto them again. He certainly seemed to have his vitality back now.

When finally they parted again, he was looking at her with eyes as full of life and spirit as ever.

"Are you restored?" Tayarene hoped softly.

There was a twinkle again in his dark eye. "Most entirely," he asserted with quiet complacence.

She was filled with glad relief. "So it wasn't ineffective after all," she remarked, then eyed him sagaciously. "Did you just say that to get me to kiss you again?"

He grew a slight smile. "Maybe."

She scoffed incredulously, lightly flapping the back of a hand on his chest. "Don't scare me like that," she protested in a murmur. But she was smiling too, and their eyes still met tenderly, with their faces so near.

"I just needed an extra dose of

you," he confessed softly.

Her heart glowed with warmth, and she nestled her head contentedly on his shoulder. It was a great comfort to know, with the utmost certainty, that theirs was a match of true love. Their success in averting the spell served as irrefutable proof.

Then she turned thoughtful. "But, if it was you all along...how did you find me?"

Rizorian paused with a wry quirk to his mouth. "Mezuthelion pointed you out to me."

Tayarene glanced at him in surprise. Mezuthelion had been in on it?

"He and I have known each other for years. I told him about my curse, and he set to work trying to discover the one who could break it. Turns out, it was you. I couldn't tell you, or it might have changed whether you developed any feelings for me naturally."

"Why did you come to me in your animal forms first?"

"You needed to know every side of me," he explained. "To love me for all that I truly was. Otherwise, the kiss might not have worked."

"Then how come you never changed into an animal before me?"

Rizorian was sober. "It was all those rumours of the monster. A person shapeshifting into a creature might've seemed all too alarming. I didn't want to scare you off."

Tayarene smiled teasingly. "I don't scare easy."

Rizorian smiled, too. "I know that, now." He stroked the back of a finger up and down her bare shoulder. "I might've guessed, what with you chasing after

85

hooligans and such."

Little had she suspected that the fish she'd saved had actually been Rizorian! Now that she thought about it, if she hadn't pursued Suziri, she might not have dumped the fish as a distraction. "I'm so glad those hunters didn't get to you," she murmured. She wouldn't only have lost her animal companion, but the human love of her life.

Rizorian drew her a little closer. "I have you to thank for that," he said softly. "And so much more."

Now that the sun had dried their clothes and warmed them, they sat up and rose to their feet. They started strolling homeward, and Rizorian sidled his hand over to hold hers. Tayarene linked her fingers with his.

"Thanks for helping me figure out levitating, by the way. It really came in handy."

"Well, if you ever need a wizard's familiar," he began playfully, "you know where to find me."

The End

www.ingramcontent.com/pod-product-compliance
Lightning Source LLC
Chambersburg PA
CBHW071541100726
47908CB00004B/1464